Book design by Emily Horne

Published by BreadPig
breadpig.com

These comics can also be found on:
asofterworld.com

First Edition October 2015

ISBN 978-0-9828537-6-4

10 9 8 7 6 5 4 3 2 1

Printed in China

ANATOMY OF MELANCHOLY

the best of
A Softer World

Emily Horne and Joey Comeau

INTRODUCTION

Sometimes getting out of bed is the first mistake of the day. Sometimes it's the first mistake of every day. Sometimes it goes on being the case that the things you can fix are exhausted by this kind of list: Buy toilet paper. Replace light bulb.

René Char said: *Comment vivre sans inconnu devant soi?*

Suddenly life offers up a surprise! You think: That stove is filthy! I know, I'll clean the stove!!!!! See? Things weren't so bad. Your future wasn't all mapped out. That stove was just sitting there all along, offering novelty, agency, the promise of a new and better life–one with a gleaming kitchen appliance! *L'chaim!*

This kind of time is a good kind of time to turn to *A Softer World*. It's not taboo to think replacing light bulbs is not much of an incentive to get out of bed, but cutting short iterations of light bulb replacement cannot be seen as the logical next step: decency requires a lot of *Sturm und Drang*. Turn to *A Softer World* and you find logic isn't so scandalous after all.

Besides, *ASW* reminds us, there's hope!

Maybe Samaritans are simply not considering the full range of options. Maybe things would look better if someone else were dispatched to that undiscovered country from whose bourne no traveller returns. (Samaritans tend not to offer this suggestion.) Or maybe the problem is just that life is a) too predictable and b) not edited for length. But *ASW* is completely unpredictable: there are vampires, zombies, werewolves, demon babies, talking cats. There's a fern disguised as a fern. There are no continuous characters – a speaker gets three panels, six max, to strut and fret its ten seconds upon the page, and then is seen no more. It's an atomised world, a world of brilliant fragments, a world where pieties are punctured with evil glee.

Why wouldn't this be a good time to write an introduction to *A Softer World*'s greatest hits? Ah. Rashly getting out of bed every day for three weeks in a row (madness! madness!), I start making notes. Twenty pages of notes looked something like this:

279: Now my kitty won't

eat her regular food

If I'd known this would

be such a hassle

I would've just

buried that kid I found

[Black and white. Panel One, a girl, soft focus, bends down toward something out of the frame. Panel Two, a louvred door, dark beyond. Panel Three, girl and door in same frame – photo from which Panels One and Two, cropped differently.]

291: I woke up and

everyone on Earth

was gone.

This is going to be

like a nightmare

any day now

[Black and white. Panel One, place setting at table for one, very dark. Panel 2, extension of One, showing more place settings. Panel Three, extension of Two, napkin, tablecloth.]

1194: All anyone talks about

are the elaborately staged

psycho-sexual murders

I also have

a dog-walking company

[colour photograph of black Labrador on pale blue path bordered by green bushes, split into three panels, dog at far right divided between Panels Two and Three. Panel One shows only path with bushes, Panel Two path with hind leg of dog, Panel Three with rest of dog]

So. Notes. This is not enlightening. Would more examples help? No. (2:27 pm. This might be a good time to go back to bed.) Meanwhile Ryan North posts his tribute to *ASW* on Tumblr. (Curses! Curses! And we did not go back to bed why, again, exactly?) The reason this is not necessarily a good time to write about the genius of *A Softer World*? A mind honed by, erm, iterated light bulb replacement is not the weapon of choice for doing justice to its elusive sophistication. So, right. *Reculer pour mieux sauter.*

A Softer World is a collaboration which is also a division of labour: Emily Horne took photographs, Joey Comeau wrote text (not necessarily in that order). The result is profoundly unsettling, *unheimlich*, in a way that goes beyond its dark humour.

The form of the texts never varies: they are typed on cut up white strips, like notes from a kidnapper, a blackmailer, a serial killer, plastered across a world whose rules we think we know. (The speaker may just be a kid who wished their father let them have a dog, but the form aligns the sad, the lonely, the alienated with the style of monsters.) But the photographs rejoice in an extraordinary diversity of subject, style, palette, expressiveness. There are still lifes and action shots, there are claustrophobic interiors, triumphalist buildings, moody landscapes; adorable animals; crowds, solitaries, faces in obsessive, obtrusive close-up, humans aggressively cropped (think the shoot-out in *The Good, the Bad, and the Ugly*) to eyes, ear, hand, a shoe. There are nondescript patches of grass. There are panels in love with colour – a dark, dense, saturated blue, the blithe frivolous pink of a flowering tree, the burnt orange of a plausible fern. There are panels like the ostensively uncontrived casual snapshot, panels embracing the overt artifice of advertising, film. (It would be fatally easy to go on.)

The photographs are never simply illustrations of the 'story', though the speaker sometimes appears; the reader finds, instead, a tension between two kinds of narrative time. The ruthless economy of the texts follows the sequential framework of a joke: set-up, exposition, punchline, kicker in the mouseover. The division of the strip into three, sometimes six frames reinforces this, the visual implication is that the photographs also show different stages of the 'action'. But the frames are often obviously simply slices of the same photograph – either a single image cut in sections, or an image shown at a distance before a single detail is seen in close-up (or vice versa). (The dog is always, obviously, attached to its tail; it is not a narrative development, or even a reveal, when a frame with the dog's hind leg is followed by a frame with the rest of the dog.) What's going on?

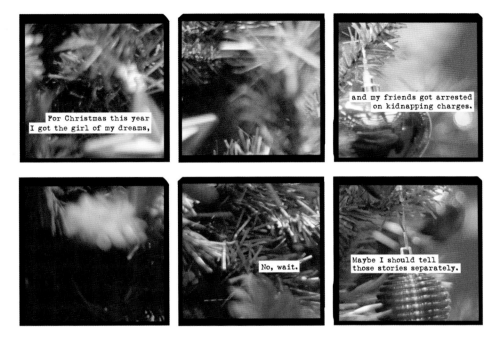

For Christmas this year
I got the girl of my dreams,

and my friends got arrested
on kidnapping charges.

No, wait.

Maybe I should tell
those stories separately.

Why is it funnier, more subversive, to cut up a single image of the tree in six pieces? To use two frames of this static image to introduce pauses? The pauses are, of course, essential to the joke's perfect timing – as is giving "No, wait" a frame to itself – but those bits of tree aren't pauses in the action of a tree, or even a Western Front where all was ironically quiet (nothing was going on in any part of the tree, at any time). So, why?

As I say, the dull brain perplexes and retards. But…I think there's an energy in the obstinacy, the intransigence of the elements. They work together, sure – like Tuco and Blondie. They have their own agendas.

We live in a world of images saturated not only with RGB/CYMK but with meaning, and, after a while, everything we see looks like part of a story we already know. *Comment vivre sans inconnu devant soi? A Softer World* is a reminder that it doesn't have to be that way. People may not always surprise you, but Joey and Emily ain't people. (And you should keep that fern under surveillance.)

If that isn't genius, it'll have to do, until—but no. The real thing has come along.

Helen DeWitt
June 2015, Berlin

Are my parents ever coming home?

Baby Doom knew that they all had to die

but after they died,

who would change him? who would feed him?

There had to be an answer

There had to be an answer.

In the caves behind my house I found a softer world.

They understand what I had to do for love.

They don't believe in restraining orders.

what I did for love

a softer world

I lost my whole family to the fire.

I cried for weeks. Nothing could console me.

Until I woke up this morning, and I could fly.

Just spread my arms and go.

just go.

The mayor says be calm. Waters rise, and towns flood.

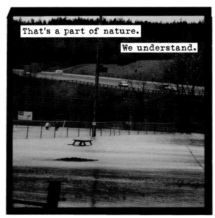

That's a part of nature. We understand.

We do not understand the giant babies.

care to explain THAT one?

anatomy of melancholy

13

There are people who believe a photo captures your soul.

For them this is a terrible thing.

For me it's one last chance.

He never meant for it to end.

He wanted to give her everything.

So when she said "Higher," he pushed her higher.

But she said "No. Higher."

a softer world

One year for mother's day
my mother took me
to the beach

and left.

I have this dream

where my sister is

taking my picture,

and I keep saying

don't get on that plane

and she says

say cheese

anatomy of melancholy

It's too late now.

Millions of bottles
are already
on the shelves.

Every one of them a winner.

I laugh along,

but inside I know
that it's true:

Being in love
is totally punk rock.

a softer world

yes, I believe in love,
yes, I'm a dreamer.

but I'm not alone.

there are more of us
than you suspect,

and we've got bombs.

truth and beauty bombs.

anatomy of melancholy   17

a puddle in a basement grew and grew,

and the whole town rushed to save fax machines and public records

while I rolled up my pant legs.

birds gotta fly

I should have been brave enough to just ask your name,

instead of screaming "I cannot contain my lust"

now you probably think I'm a creep.

I can contain it, if I have to.

a softer world

my dad says

sometimes things aren't
a simple dichotomy.

he tucks me in and says

sometimes doctors
are only human.

and that
I am a girl

because they flipped heads
instead of tails.

Is it a boy or a girl? Maybe.

I was so sure
my search would end

when I found god.

But then
I couldn't find
my car keys

and my cat ran away.

She was so fluffy.

anatomy of melancholy

There's a whole world
off this island.

All it takes is
one long swim
to start over.

Tell my mother I love her.

go, emily, go!

I'm afraid to go
on this mission,
afraid
of sabotage
of system failure

oh, what do I do?

but when I tried
to tell my mother

she smiled so wide
and said
"my son the astronaut"

20

a softer world

On my mom's birthday, I put on my best suit.

I get a haircut.

I pretend she's coming home.

I don't know if your wings are real,

but I've never seen you without them,

and I follow you everywhere.

anatomy of melancholy

I was going to
figure out the postage,

and send you my heart

for Christmas.

But my friends
talked me out of it.

they said
"Why would you send her
something broken?"

we've been good, but we can't last

22

a softer world

When I watch
the birds playing

I want something
and don't
know what.

I guess that means sex.

is there something wrong?

there's a creature
out there

some ancient machine
of muscle
and
scales,

that I can sell

history cudlers

anatomy of melancholy

I'm sorry

I took your beauty for granted before the accident.

I guess

it doesn't matter

now.

no, honey, you look fine

Cornered by zombies, all I can think to do

is confess.

It was me

who told dad

you were gay.

But I never told him about your best selling romance novels.

24

a softer world

ME:

SWF, 23.

YOU:

non monogamous
interested in
overthrowing
the heteronormative
ownership paradigm,

not ugly.

I told everyone
I built my robot wife

for sex

but late at night

when we're alone

we mostly play Battleship.

anatomy of melancholy   25

Out in the yard, birds were coming back from the dead.

They were too slow to fly,

lumbering toward their victims

chirping "braaaaaaaaains..."

hen there's no more room in pigeon hell...

We bet him five dollars that he would drown.

A bittersweet victory.

and you'll look stupid then!

a softer world

Terrorists attacked
and I called my sister

She said it was
too much drama

before
her morning coffee

and hung up on me.

I meant to suicide

but the warm water
was your voice

and I touched myself
instead

anatomy of melancholy

maybe next year

is the year

maybe 1996 was

maybe last year

when I played "doctor"

this is Emily and she is so pretty

I played to win

a softer world

I like falling off
my skateboard

the way i like loving you

broken hearts,
like broken bones

hurt well

He said

"You make my heart stop"

and I blushed, flattered

when I should have been
calling nine one one

anatomy of melancholy

email me dirty pictures
of you with my name
in marker everywhere

i get crazy thinking
about your eyes when you cry

i miss you all wrong.

The trick to pet names
is the combination
of affectionate nouns

Honeybun.

Sugarpie.

Kittentits.

a softer world

I have superpowers
and a costume
Every night I panic
just outside my door
But every night
I try again

what if people don't want my help?

My mom's buried
out in these woods.
She wanted her ashes
scattered at sea
but it's like she always said
"No."

it just wasn't reasonable

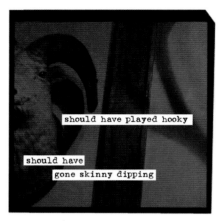
should have played hooky

should have gone skinny dipping

should have asked Maureen to the forest prom.

my daughter is a terrorist.

a mother knows.

she is my little girl, though.

those people are strangers.

a softer world

I've always known I'd be a bank robber.

So judge all you want, ladies and gentlemen.

Because you never did become an astronaut.

the newspapers made a big deal about my heritage

but ignored my tattoo

"fuck politics I just want to burn shit down"

anatomy of melancholy

Gandhi said
"be the change
you want to see
in the world,"

fuck that

be the trouble
you want to see
in the world

work is a vampire
that sucks me dry

which is a metaphor

but still the reason
I stuck a chair leg
through my manager

a softer world

i FREEDOM FIGHTER BOMBING love you whether you reply or JIHAD not

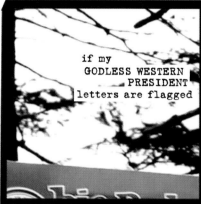

if my GODLESS WESTERN PRESIDENT letters are flagged

our love will outlive us in their SUBWAY SARIN GAS computers

even after we're done

since the baby, my wife she has depression, so I am having a fake affair

"Honey I'm late again, don't you want to scream or yell

or get out of bed?"

oh no, is that lipstick on my collar?

anatomy of melancholy

oh god, oh god.

okay. calm down.
say something.
break the ice.
set her at ease.

"I'm unarmed."

because, uh, you might have heard I run with a dangerous crowd?

I have no use for
"before and after"
pictures.

I can't remember starting, and

I'm never done.

to die would be an awfully big adventure

36

a softer world

I spend my lunch hours surrounded by people, who apologize for every touch,

so today I hugged a stranger

and a thousand lonely people rioted

I couldn't stop smiling in the back of the police car.

Truth and Beauty are wonderful words

but shrapnel is shrapnel

and at the end of the day

I am alone with the things I have done.

we buried truth under playgrounds

anatomy of melancholy

This is the fifth afternoon
we've spent just making cupcakes

maybe we didn't survive
that crash

another mario 3 tournament tonight, ladies?

I brought you back to life
picturing chaos and excitement
not to be
your brains delivery girl.

Get off your ass
if you're hungry,

you lazy zombie fuck.

I don't care what Proust said. Fuck you. How about that.

a softer world

We are terrible for each other, and, yes we are a disaster.

But tell me your heart doesn't race for a hurricane or a burning building.

I'd rather die terrified

than live forever.

mistakes aren't always regrets

My mother always said,
"a life needs solid plans,"

but really

a life needs secret plans.

saying your plans out loud is a good way to hear god laugh

a friend will help you move

I wish I were close with my mother

a best friend will
help you move bodies

but if you have to move
your best friend's body
you're on your own

a softer world

I woke up in the woods covered in blood

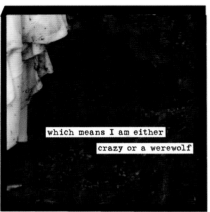

which means I am either crazy or a werewolf

but I'm not a nobody

My mom used to say. "Hell's where the party will be!"

Nope.

anatomy of melancholy

home is where the heart is

until we get a chance
to bury it

out back is where the toes are

I said I would
never leave you

but come on.

What are you, new?

I would die without you? Seriously?

42

a softer world

anatomy of melancholy

since my orgasm
I forget faces,
and confuse words,

but I can head injury now

so, fifty fifty?

thirty-seventy, really.

I like to wear a wig
and ride elevators.

I smile at businessmen
until they get out,

then I stage whisper,
"Target is on the move.
Ninth floor."

drop outs have more fun

44

a softer world

if at first
you don't succeed,

run.

Death is coming and
we've been making charts,
wasting time.

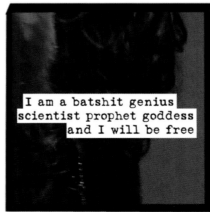

I am a batshit genius
scientist prophet goddess
and I will be free

and I guess this message is
to let you know that
I won't be in tomorrow.

anatomy of melancholy

They are always watching

always listening

recording everything.

So I sing into the phone, sometimes.

Maybe it cheers them up.

lullabies at night, george michael in the morning

a softer world

The carbon footprint of a single human being is enormous

If you think about it, your honour,

I'm an environmentalist.

relocation ships came down through permanent smog to save us from the exploding sun

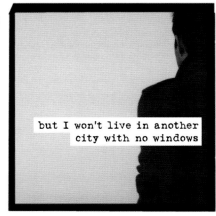

but I won't live in another city with no windows

I'd rather die with the sun on my face.

anatomy of melancholy

I can switch at will between being a man or a woman.

It's not my problem if you get weirded out

because my body stays the same.

any sufficiently complex system is hackable

I never wanted anything to happen to my parents

but a hero needs an origin story.

and I'm not even sure gamma radiation would do anything.

a softer world

If I could only bring three things to a desert island,

all three would be you.

And I'd make you all kiss.

then who's gay, smartass?

I am sick of the jokes.

Oh, ha ha. A cowboy who still lives with his mom.

But she needs me.

We can go to the rodeo after I pick up her medicine.

anatomy of melancholy

Two roads diverged in a wood, and I-

I just picked one because who cares?

we were so drunk we'd fuck anywhere

sorry I could not travel both, and be one traveler

The first joke every idiot makes is "which one of you is the dad?"

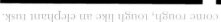

I guess it's me, though.

I'm the one who always punches the prick

and regrets it.

come rough, tough like an elephant tusk.

50

a softer world

there are no
sweeter words
than this.

nothing lasts forever.

Sure, play another song. I've got nothing better to do.

when you are
feeling low

I will be there
to feel you up.

anatomy of melancholy

51

Yes. Yes I am the fluffiest kitty oh my gosh ever.

And every day I learn how to make myself smarter and fluffier.

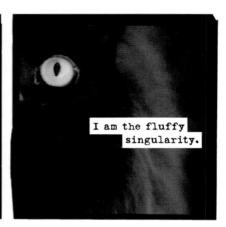

I am the fluffy singularity.

No, I don't want to be a woman.

What a stupid, misguided idea of homosexuality!

I want you to be the woman.

52

a softer world

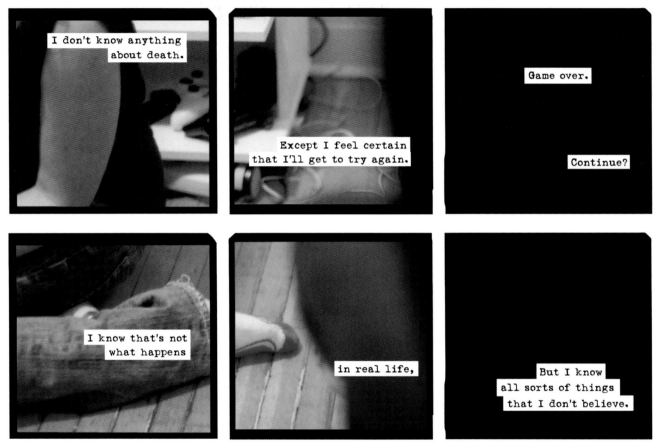

Continue?

anatomy of melancholy

The aliens have come bearing gift after gift of amazing technology

only, this time it is hover beads.

and I'm down there every day with some beads and a sign:

We're falling for our own trick.

"Girl Genius turned Girl Slut in these exclusive photos!"

What's that? I can't hear you.

But you know that sex doesn't actually make people dumber, right?

Let's hear you laugh without oxygen, world!

I used to hope for the apocalypse.

Now there is no hope at all.

now the collection agencies have armies.

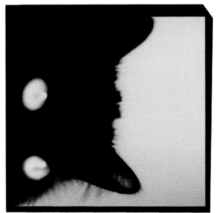

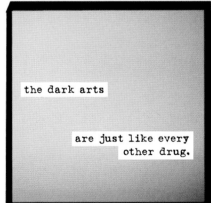

the dark arts

are just like every other drug.

not so interesting after you find out your mom does it.

jesus, mom. I have friends coming over.

The lake creature knows we are hunting her,

but she also knows

we are the first in years.

the beast may try to hug you.

I cannot help but notice we are

sitting-in-a-tree.

I want us to gerund, essentially.

So, you know, maybe we could think of something to do...

verb-wise.

a softer world

my last words will be, 'yeah, I had that coming.'

Sex and respect
go together like

you and me, please.

If that's what you're into.

Better to have loved and lost

than to wake up
next to you every day.

Only love can break your heart.

58

a softer world

When I was just a little girl

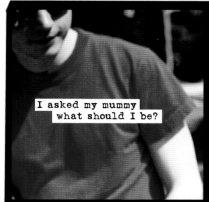

I asked my mummy what should I be?

"Fuck 'should'," she said

my last words will be, 'yeah, I had that coming.'

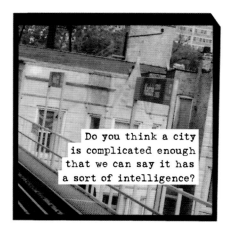

Do you think a city is complicated enough that we can say it has a sort of intelligence?

No, I don't care where you work.

No, YOU are the worst speed date here.

More importantly, who is your favourite Muppet?

anatomy of melancholy

I have found a way to watch video in your head.

High definition, with instant replay.

It is called having regrets.

Why do I do this? Oh god. So much chocolate milk.

Give me liberty.

I do not feel that you should have a second opinion here.

wait, give me liberty or give YOU death. how about that?

a softer world

I always thought violence didn't solve anything.

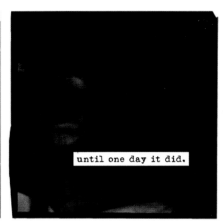

until one day it did.

and the guilt I expected never came.

Life would be way easier if I were easier.

Fact.

A stranger's just

a friend

you probably won't like.

Yeah. Probably.

I want to rob lumber mills and hospitals with you

and just bewilder the hell out of people

the way love should.

We will make everything wrong in the right way.

a softer world

You and me

and baby makes

life into a string of compromises.

Maybe the Earth would be better off without us.

Safe and clean and perfect

like a toy nobody ever played with.

anatomy of melancholy

I have never had a kid complain about swearing.

So if you're firing me,

I assume it was their shit cunt parents.

I wish seeing you naked

was as good

as wishing I could see you naked.

a softer world

Moderation is like

a foreign language.

You have to learn that shit

when you're young.

sexually transmitted infections are like

hangovers.

they're not great,

but neither is moderation.

anatomy of melancholy

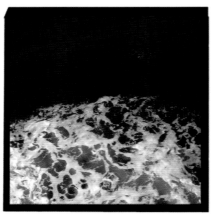

I wish I could walk a mile in your shoes

right out into the ocean

Do you have to play that harp at 3am? Really?

This is indeed an exciting time for fuel cell research,

but before we get started on these slides,

do you guys ever get sad?

yeah, me neither.

a softer world

My parents made sure
I had a good work ethic.

ROYAL TR

I still hate working,

ST TOWER

but when I'm not working
I hate myself.

Trouble is my business,

and business is
my middle name.

How much should I
put you down for?

anatomy of melancholy

I asked for a fairytale romance.

In my defense, I'd never read any actual fairy tales.

First time I've ever wished for a disney version.

I'm a poet

Maybe I'll learn the acoustic guitar instead.

and I didn't know it

would make me so obnoxious.

a softer world

The answer is obvious.

We blow up the moon.

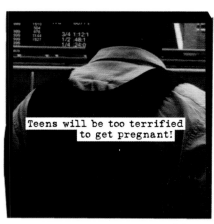

Teens will be too terrified to get pregnant!

Many problems. One solution. No moon by 2030.

I used my one wish to make myself smarter.

Smart enough to wish I was more kind.

won't you believe it it's just my luck

I wonder if
the ugly duckling

felt stupid

when he realized

being pretty

didn't magically
solve all his problems

of course he got no sympathy from the ducklings that were still ugly.

Here lies Joey Comeau

he left the world
the way he entered it:

covered in placenta.

oh no, not again

a softer world

Look. I'm just being honest.

That excuses me from empathy or tact, right?

Any asshole can tell the truth.

I wish there was

a better word

than 'sorry.'

But then I'd probably need a better word than that.

cunnilingus? a...analingus?

anatomy of melancholy

I disagree with
your opinion

but I will defend
to the death

your right

to go fuck yourself.

Check outside. I think you'll find you have sufficient space.

I figure you are already

pretty badly off

if "May you lead an
interesting life,"

sounds like a curse to you.

Plenty of time to be a boring fuck in the grave.

a softer world

If you don't have anything nice to say

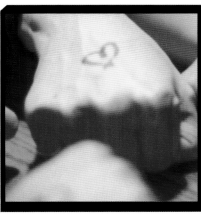

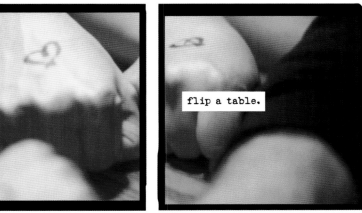

flip a table.

Fuck this table and fuck you!

I wonder how many hauntings go unreported

because wailing and the clank of chains

are still better than an empty house.

and now I have an excuse to buy new sheets all the time!

You are the love of my
life so far.

Plenty of time to be a boring fuck in the grave.

You make me want

to pretend
to be a better man.

I promise, I'm going to seem to do right by you.

a softer world

Good decisions are just

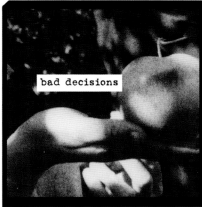

bad decisions

you didn't get to make.

I love the way
your face lights up

when someone says,

"It might be dangerous."

anatomy of melancholy

Live and learn

or die and teach by example.

that is too many words to tattoo on your penis

There should be a word for the things we do

In bed.

not because we want to

but because we want to be the kind of person who wants to.

a softer world

Sex doesn't ruin friendships,

people ruin friendships.

post hoc, ergo propter hoc

I finally developed a computer with feelings.

It just doesn't have feelings for me.

it's in love with randall munroe.

anatomy of melancholy

Go on, guess.

Guess whose shit
I am totally sick of.

how come
being easy

keeps getting

harder?

78

a softer world

If you died,
I would go through hell
to bring you back.

That would be easy.

I'm not sure how to deal
with us just

drifting apart.

our dark long aphty

Don't think of it
as us breaking up.

think of it as

me being happy again.

now get out of the bushes before I call the cops.

anatomy of melancholy

79

A woman's love is like a big spider.

Super gross.

maybe I am doing it wrong?

I joined Plenty of Fish to find out who stole my bike.

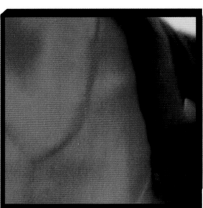

A fun first date would be going to your house

to see if you have my bike.

What a lovely home. Do you have a shed?

80

a softer world

Sometimes when someone says,
"go big or go home,"

it's kind of nice
to just go home.

If you can't stand the heat, turn the A/C on.

Do you know why
you never read about
suicides in the newspaper?

Because it isn't news.

there's a darkness on the edge of town.

anatomy of melancholy

Sometimes when two people love each other

it's really unfortunate.

she looks like one of those rap guys' girlfriends

It freaks me out when I think about how big the universe is.

Just so big and growing bigger, exploding outward constantly in all directions.

So no, I don't care how fast I was going, officer.

A ticket? We're HURTLING THROUGH THE VOID!!

a softer world

I love you the way

a knife loves a heart

the way a bomb loves a crowd

the way your mother
warned you about,
essentially.

the way a human loves another human

Spare the axe,

spoil the child.

I think we should fire that babysitter.

anatomy of melancholy

You can't fire me,

and this is why.

I quit

I quit like a year ago.

It's time
to make yourself proud

don't you know? the sun's setting fast.

and everyone else
a little nervous.

a softer world

Citizens should not fear their government.

This will be enforced.

I only got one law. A kid who tells on another kid is a dead kid.

I believe most people are inherently good.

But overcoming our nature

is what separates us from the animals.

evil has its pleasures too.

I'm going to dress up like a sexy orphan for halloween!

I have the outfit,

now I just need to kill my parents.

I hope they don't read my blog.

Civilization is the ability to distinguish

what you like

from what you like to watch pornography of.

And anyway why were you going through my computer?

86

a softer world

I wish I could say that it gets better,

but my jaw is still wired shut.

Marriage isn't just between a man and a woman

it's between any two people who love each other

and want to ruin their lives.

in front of jesus and everybody.

anatomy of melancholy

Overreaction:

Any reaction to something that doesn't affect me.

Have you tried walking it off?

You were my everything,

which, upon reflection,

was probably the problem.

A cautionary tale, but at least it was X-rated.

a softer world

Nothing matters at all.

Might as well be nice to people.

Hand out your chuckles while you can.

No offence, but

I am glad that we're friends.

I wish I could eat your cancer when you turn black.

anatomy of melancholy

I hate it when you leave

but I love to look
at your butt
while you walk away.

it gives me sexual arousal.

It's later than you think.

Go ahead and fuck up.

Who has time for perfection?

90

a softer world

I might tire myself out from struggling,

and drown

but I will not sink.

I fought my way into this world. I'll fight my way out.

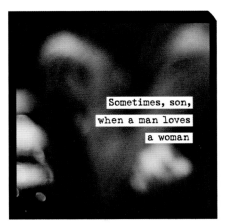

Sometimes, son, when a man loves a woman

he gets sort of creepy.

Man, I'm totally stuck in the 'nice guy who acts creepy' zone.

anatomy of melancholy

It broke my heart
when I realized

my father had a whole
secret second family

and that they
got to have a dog.

Did he ever really love us?

Everybody dies.

Every single person.

So,
style counts.

Is that what you're wearing?

92   a softer world

If poetry could describe

the way you make me feel

poetry would be illegal.

Or anyway I might get arrested.

Do you ever get the feeling
that God has a plan?

And you're the only one

who can stop it?

yippee ki yay, YHWH

anatomy of melancholy

I don't mean to sound
like a creep,

but I've seen you around

and I wrote a book about
what if you were
a sexy pirate.

What if Ryan North were a sexy pirate? THE BOOK.

Death is not the end.

Death is an ocean
on all sides of   our lives.

Deep and dark and cold,
and anything but empty.

the shuffle of crabs on the ocean floor

a softer world

When I look at you,

I can't help but think

Hell must be missing an angel.

did it hurt? when you clawed your way up from the depths of hell?

Having all the answers

just means you've been

asking boring questions.

the freedom of uncertainty.

anatomy of melancholy

She turned me down.

She's probably a lesbian,

or a person with her own life and interests I guess.

Cock tease: (n) Person with sexual interests distinct from mine.

When someone says, "I don't read,"

the flirting is over.

and the hunt begins.

96

a softer world

Our love is   a forest fire

and we are
the little things

that live in the trees.

Today is the most exciting last day of our lives.

Give a man a fish
and he'll eat for a day.

Teach a man to murder
people who teach him things

and you're fucked.

What were you THINKING?!

anatomy of melancholy

If every possible universe

exists somewhere
in the infinity
of space and time,

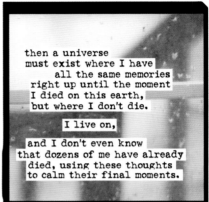

then a universe
must exist where I have
all the same memories
right up until the moment
I died on this earth,
but where I don't die.

I live on,

and I don't even know
that dozens of me have already
died, using these thoughts
to calm their final moments.

Infinity as she is played.

We sabotaged a whole factory
of magic eight balls,

so they only tell the truth.

We are all fucked,

and we are all saved.

outlook SO GOOD

a softer world

Our love was doomed,
a burning building,
a broken neck.

But nothing since
you and me

even feels like love.

I spend all my time in puddles. I miss the ocean.

We talk in the dark
as we fall asleep,

and we are objects in
the night sky

outside of time.

it is the exact opposite of alone.

anatomy of melancholy

Will you still love me

when I am a spooky ghost?

yes, Yes, always, yes.

I think I've got fireflies

where my caution should be.

Instead of slowing down, I just shine brighter.

a softer world

Girl, you're the light of my life.

The future's so bright.

anatomy of melancholy

The people who
make the least

have to put up
with the most.

what you get for choosing poor parents

The government listens
to everyone, everywhere.

Maybe I should
date them instead.

at least they'd know what I like in bed.

a softer world

I know I want love,
but I have no idea

who will make me happy.

Emptiness doesn't know
its own shape.

For a long time I thought
I deserved better

but the truth is

we both deserve better
than this.

anatomy of melancholy

When life gives you lemons

take the lemons
and be thankful
you got anything.

And then go home to your empty apartment.

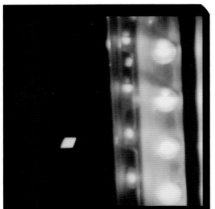

When life gives you lemons,
be cool.

It's just the drugs.

Just smile. Just keep smiling a bit longer.

a softer world

anatomy of melancholy

CAN'T STOP

WON'T STOP

NOT SURE HOW TO STOP

WHY STOP

Ah, unrequited love.

Participation medals of the heart.

When your best isn't enough.

a softer world

I hate to see you leave

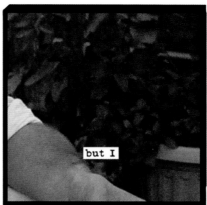

but I

kind of hate it when you're here, too.

after you're gone is nice

I'm not looking for a soul mate.

I've never believed in the majesty

of caged animals.

The sublime tigress has another nap, because who cares.

anatomy of melancholy

There are just

two things

that make life worth living.

The people you love,

and sweet pranks.

Haha a toilet full of bees! You guys are the best!

a softer world

Love is a drawer

for knives to rust in.

I'm a knife, knifin' around, cut cut cut cut cut cut cut.

Looking at you is like
looking in a mirror

except I like what I see.

I would never break your heart, seven years bad luck!

anatomy of melancholy

it takes two people

to make sex good

but only one spider

to make it terrible

four legs good, eight legs bad.

Marriage,

the ultimate double dare.

neither of us chose truth

a softer world

I used to believe
in spirits, in demons.

I don't know if they
abandoned me,

or I abandoned them.

the woods are just trees, and I am lost

I have loved

since you.

But when the new paint
gets scratched,

there you are
underneath.

My heart is layers of scar.

when you're near

the creatures inside me go still and quiet

and watch you from behind my eyes.

i have never seen them scared before

If I ever get murdered

don't tell the cops a goddamn thing.

It's what I would have wanted.

they don't care cause they stay paid anyway

a softer world

Happiness is not

a house where you can live.

but it is a house you can build.

When people say

our love won't

last forever

it sounds like they think

anything will.

I just smile and say, 'compared to what?'

anatomy of melancholy

At my worst, I worry you'll realize

you deserve better.

At my best, I worry you won't.

I'm tied to the tracks.

But I don't need you to rescue me.

I need you to be the train.

a softer world

Don't love someone

to save yourself.

Love someone to destroy who you used to be.

Everyone smiles at us, like we're the cutest couple.

Let's do something wrong.

anatomy of melancholy

Had a job

predicting the future.

Got fired for crying.

didn't even bring lunch that day.

Do not be ashamed of your secrets.

I can't imagine a lion who thinks starving

is better than someone watching them kill.

You shouldn't be afraid they will see the real you. They should be.

116

a softer world

I used to think

being intelligent
was enough.

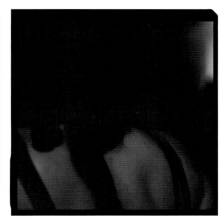

i got mine.

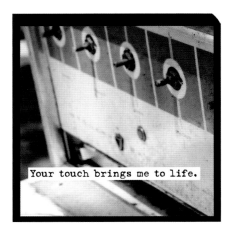
Your touch brings me to life.

Not like Frankenstein,

like HAL.

I'm half crazy, all for the love of you

Some friends you see every day,

and some friends you see when there's blood in the air.

You need both.

Your daytime friends are no help in the dark.

sex is like a beautiful sunset, the whole sky on fire,

and then, screaming through the flames,

your mother rides a skeleton horse.

and you hear her mournful cry

a softer world

Sometimes two people can love each other,

even though one is a wrist

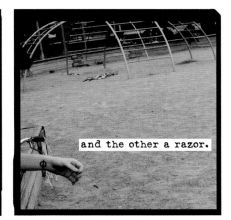

and the other a razor.

my five year plan

is to maybe go out for ice cream

this afternoon?

anatomy of melancholy

Live every day

like the cops

have no idea.

TO CHASM ⇧

They probably don't!

Live every day

like you already died

be quiet, is what i'm saying

120

a softer world

Live every day

like your mom

said it was alright.

I already asked mine.

I am surprised
more suicide notes

don't just say,
"No thank you."

I'd rather not.

 we carry our own

 loneliness

 with us

It isn't some creepy haunted doll, just showing up. You PACKED it.

 Such trivialities do not even register to me.

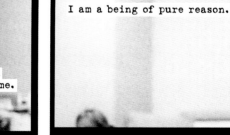 I am a being of pure reason.

 Love would only slow me down.

and anyway your kisses were stupid

a softer world

Doctors hate me! I don't blame them. I'm garbage.

I would die for you. But then again, I like dying.

anatomy of melancholy

How's life?

Well, I'm getting back what I put into it.

So, not great.

love is stupid.

happiness is admitting

we aren't better than stupid.

a softer world

Homewrecker, noun.

Someone who frees
an injured animal
from a trap.

Go! Run! You're free!

I used to say I missed you
after just a weekend.

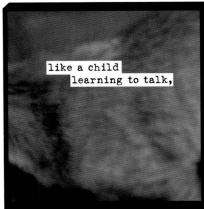

like a child
learning to talk,

who calls every cat a tiger.

And now what words do I have?

anatomy of melancholy

If loud weird public sex is wrong,

then being wrong

is wicked hot.

dare to be stupid

chosen by Kickstarter backer Sean 'Ariamaki' Riedinger!

a softer world

The end will come

like an iceberg

and I will help

everyone else

into the lifeboats

hiding my relief
behind a hero's mask

selflessly getting what I wanted

love is a dream

someone else had
last night.

no I don't want to hear about your dream

anatomy of melancholy

Remember when
your potential

was a promise

instead of a regret?

potential is just a promise you break to yourself

In the caves behind my house
I found the ruins

of a softer world.

Kindness couldn't save them.

Kindness won't save anyone.

a softer world

Maybe cats will take over when we all die.

That's a nice thought.

I hope we all die.

oh man! remember PEOPLE?!

If you put your mind to it

you can do anything.

But you won't.

and you'll feel bad because you could've.

There are some secrets
I will take to my grave.

But I don't want loving you

to be one of them.

this, at least, is up to me.

130

a softer world

The sun is shining

and the birds are singing

and because today

is the very last day

they will sing forever.

listen while you can

anatomy of melancholy

I GUESS IT REALLY WAS...
A SOFTER WORLD

I started my comic, *Dinosaur Comics*, on February 1st, 2003. Joey Comeau and Emily Horne started *A Softer World* six days later, and not too long afterwards, Joey emailed me. "What are you going to do with your Nobel Prize for Comics money?" he asked. "My name's Joey. I do a comic too."

I followed his link and read all the comics there in one sitting. They were hilarious and sad, sometimes at the same time, and I saw stuff done in comics that I hadn't seen before. I remember this one in particular, because it is the one where I mentally recategorized the series from "this is good" to "okay, this is great":

I wrote him back and asked him what he was going to do with his Pulitzer Prize for Comics money.

That was nearly thirteen years ago.

I have two friends who are marrying each other, only one of them's an American, and there's a part of the immigration process they have to convince the Canadian federal government that theirs is a real relationship. They have been directed to collect essays from people wherein we swear we know them, and to demonstrate our Friendship Credentials, we go over our relationship with one or both of them and explain why this friendship is real and important to us.

What we have to do, in effect, is write an essay - just like in school! - only the subject is why my two friends who are marrying each other are so great. It's a friendship love letter, and it was so satisfying to write. There's no time in our culture where we are allowed to walk up to our friends and say "Our friendship is so amazing, and so important to me, and I wrote an essay about it. I hope you enjoy it," except for this one, created by an immigration bureaucracy. I think we should change that.

a softer world

Joey and I emailed back and forth almost daily for several months until one time he was in Halifax while my girlfriend Priya was visiting, and I insisted they meet. I hadn't met him in person yet, but I'd already told her all about him. I told her she had to go meet my internet friend. They went out for breakfast, and when the bill came, Joey just looked at the bill and smiled wide. Priya picked up the tab. Then he got her to push him home on his skateboard. This story makes sense when you realize how much of a charmer Joey is. Priya said she loved him! I wasn't surprised. "Joey's so great," I said.

I started grad school, which meant moving to Toronto where I didn't know anyone. Joey emailed his friends Tim and Ro and got them to invite me to a games night they were having. Listen: I was young. I was excited. I showed up early and rang their doorbell at 6pm for a 8:30pm games night, because I had no idea what I was doing.

Tim and Ro invited this complete stranger in to join them at dinner that night, and it turned out they were awesome, and now just about everyone I know in Toronto can be traced back to Tim and Ro and those weekly games nights they hosted. What Joey gave me through Tim and Ro was a friendship starter kit, a way to make moving to a new city easy, and when my books got water damaged during the move, Joey sent me new ones. All his favourites.

I love him, and we would've never met if it weren't for *A Softer World*.

anatomy of melancholy

There will always be people taunting me

laughing because I tower above them,

a giant.

Pointing with fingers that have never touched a cloud

Emily and I disagree over how we met in real life, but that's great because now we have a mystery at the centre of our friendship. There's a sequence of events where I say one thing happened and she says "no you're crazy THAT'S IMPOSSIBLE", but I can't even remember what our two different versions are anymore. Mine is absolutely the right one though.

One of my earliest memories of her is of being at Tim's housewarming for his new place, and in his kitchen he'd left this seltzer bottle: they're those giant pressurized water bottles clowns spray each other with, at least in cartoons I guess? And obviously at some point I sprayed Emily a little, because this is what happens when you leave me in my 20s in a kitchen at a party with a seltzer bottle. Emily sprayed me back in revenge, but it was more than I'd sprayed her, so obviously I needed to spray her back to make it even. It went back and forth until Tim burst into his kitchen, (understandably) mad that we'd sprayed water all over his new apartment. He told us to stop. We apologized. And as he was leaving Emily emptied the bottle on me before putting the drained bottle in Tim's hands.

Reader, I befriended her.

a softer world

One time she sent me a physical letter. A real letter! Nothing is more classy. I hung it on my wall. I bought a used typewriter at a garage sale so I could respond in kind. She moved to Toronto later on, and we started hanging out all the time. When Jenn and I got married, she photographed our wedding.

I love her, and we would've never met if it weren't for A Softer World.

Once, my comic mentioned "truth" and "beauty" and Joey and Emily's comic that day mentioned "truth and beauty bombs", so we started a message board for our comics called that. We don't post there anymore, but others do. It's still running. People got married because of that message board. Children exist today from that thing! There's a chain of events that leads from today back through our years of comics and friendship, through Joey and Emily and the way our three lives have intertwined, all the way to when we three babies started comics within the same week even though none of us can draw, and Joey emailing me to inquire about my Nobel Prize for Comics money. Without A Softer World, I never meet Joey, I never meet Emily, and my life is completely different. Probably worse, too!

It's almost definitely worse!

Congratulations, Ryan North and Jenn Klug on this, the occasion of your first wedding.

There's a dedication in the first *Dinosaur Comics* collection. It reads, "To Emily and Joey: the first friends I ever made in comics, and still the best."

I'm sad Emily and Joey's comic is ending–more than I thought I'd be, I've got all these big feelings about it you guys–but I'm glad it was there. I am here to tell you now, and without hyperbole, that this comic and the two people behind it have shaped my life more than any other work of art. Take that, the Mona Lisa.

In conclusion, *A Softer World* was so amazing, and so important to me, and I wrote an essay about it. I hope you enjoyed it.

Ryan North
May 2015, Toronto

GOLD ★ BACKERS

THANK YOU!

A C Bachmann, A. K. Tosh, A. Sheppard, A. Storkey, A.I. Ruiz-Sanabria, A.J. Penney, Aaron F. Gonzalez, Aaron Hamer, Aaron Mikolajcik, Aaron Pollock, Aaron Reichman, Aaron W, Aaron Wood, Abby Goutal, Abigail Kidd, Adam Anderson, Adam Burke, Adam Coffee, Adam Donald, Adam Freiden, Adam Greig, Adam Howe, Adam Mayes, Adam Sulek, Adan "Absolutely" Moreno, Addison Fox, Aditya Sarin, Adrian Nelson, aG, Aidan Bodsworth, Aimee & Christian E, Akasha Yi, Al, Al Tasker, Alaina Brenick, Alan Scott Belsky, Alana Duran and Tom Parkin, Albert Cua, Alec Kunkel, Alec Rundle, Alejandra Oliva, Alex Clatworthy, Alex H, Alex Hoffman, Alex Kerfoot, Alex Kolanko, Alex Orf, Alex S, Alex Scarr, Alex T, Alex Ware , Alex Weaver, Alexander Norlund, Alexander Pattenden, Alexander Sullivan, Alexandra Brumberg, Alexandra Colalillo, Alexandra Cox, Alexandra Marcil, Alexandra Shkandrij, Alexis Chaney, Alfred Newman, Ali & Robin, Alice Millward, Alice Wheeler, Alicia Castillo Holley, Alicia Duffy, Alicia Fry, Aliisa Percival, Alison Scott, Alistair Parker, Allen Hair, Allie and Lindsay MacLeod, Allie K., Allisa, Allison Rubenok, Aly DeWills-Marcano, Alysha Gallant, Alyson Julia Pygon, Alyx & Xy Ward, Amanda, Amanda, Amanda B. Delp, Amanda Clare Lees, Amanda Domino, Amanda Griggs, Amanda Killian, Amanda Lee, my dear, Amanda M. Shadiack, Amanda Shondell, Amanda Taylor, Amanda Tryon, Amber Baldet, amber dawn pullin, Amber Fermo, Amberle Browne, Amelia Fineberg, Amelia O'Leary, Amos C Hendershott, Amy Grace, Amy Slabach, Ana Miloš, anderer, Anders, Andi Carrison, Andrea Bichan, Andrea Carney, Andrea Skouras & Caz Downing-Bryant, Andrea Sliger, Andreas Fuchs, Andreas Rauer, Andrei Ligema, Andrew, Andrew, Andrew "Boter" Bugenis, Andrew Brockert, Andrew Ferguson, Andrew Hsieh, Andrew Hungerford, Andrew J Caird, Andrew James Folsom, Andrew Martin & Diane Wasser, Andrew Reid and Erin Blake, Andrew Schoenfeld, Andrew Speros, Andrew The Fury Miller, Andrew Tureski, Andrew Wright, Andy Mundy, Aneel Nazareth, Angel and Jeff Gondek, Angelie Multani, Angelina Fabbro (@ hopefulcyborg), Angie Gorospe, Ania, Ann Foreyt, Ann Harter, Ann V Call, Ann-Kathrin Niederberger, Anna Elizabeth Johnson, Anna Erkers, Anna Guiltner, Anna Isabel C. Rodriguez, Annabelle Woodger, annag, Annalise Hawney, Annalissa Roy, Anne & Miggles, Anne Schneider, Anne Walsh, Anne Williams, Annechilada, Annika Marshall, Anon, Anonymous, Anonymous, Anonymous, Anonymous, Anonymous, Ansley Barnes, Anthony A Cucinella, Anthony Farella, Anthony Rensing, Anthony Velázquez, Anthony Walsh, Anton Perc, Antonio Coelho, aoife and ryan, Aram, Araz Hashemi & Darcie Burton, Archfriend Erika Miller, Arianna Elizabeth Mayer, Ariel, Ariel Billings, Arsène Millay, Arthur Xurrath Johnson, Artur Muller, Ash Mahtani, Asher Cookson, Ashleigh Lancaster, Ashley Brookshier, Ashley Perks, Ashley Robinson, Ashley Valenzuela, Audrey M. Ha, August Johnson, Austin, Ava Grace O'Brien, Avani, Avril Kenney, Aynjel Kaye, B. Allyn Fay, b. blue marble, Banana Yoshimoto Johnson Billew Finity, Bastian, Beccy David, Belinda Duncan, Ben Cain, Ben Fowler, Ben Hughes, Ben Mohrbacher, Ben

Novack, Ben Pyman, Ben Wise, Benedict Leigh, Benjamin Cass, Benjamin David (Fox), Benjamin Franklin Craft-Rendon, Benjamin J. Guenther, Benjamin Perrault, Benjamin R. Reynolds, Benjamin Shai, Benjamin W. Silver, Berlin Kofoed, Berrak Sarikaya, Beth Bissmeyer, Beth Duffin, Beth Insko, Beth McNany, Beth Traub, Bethani Jade, Bethany Huey, Beulah Sprague-Davies, Bex Everhart, bhiller, Bill Stilwell, Bill Williams, Billy Bishop, Birdie, BJ Carter, Blair Bosserman, blank, Bliss Mellen-Ross, Blondie, Bobby Mariappuram, Bonnie-Lauren Therese Green, Brad Broge, Brad Jones, Bradley Wilson, Brady Rainey, Branden De' Boynton, Brandi Beckman, Brandi Lee, Brandon H., Braxton Meredith, Brendan Mathews, Brenny Bear, Brent Thompson, Brett, Brett Abbott, Brett Allen, Brett Bonn, Brian Elston, Brian Excarnate, Brian Ford, Brian JL Barker, Brian Kober, Brian Krulik, Brian LéRoy and Melissa Hickson, Brian Orlick, Brian Rinehart, Brian Sandford, Brian Woolsey, Brianna Walsh, Bridget M. Blodgett, bripod, Brittie Munar, Brock & Renaye, Bruno P., Bryan Henry "IMBry" Onglatco, Bryan Serrano, Bryan Zhao, Bryce, Butter Feet, BY Williams, C Meowgon, C. A. Bridges, Cael Daniel, Caitlin, Caitlin Blennerhassett, Caitlin Cedfeldt, Caitlin Rose McMonagle, Caitlin Watts-FitzGerald, Caitlyn Edwards, Caitlyn Orenshaw, Caity & Andrew Teller, Cal Wood, caleb, Caligula Verus, Callum, Cameron Bock, Cariad Eccleston, Carina Adly MacKenzie, Carl Sjostrand, Carly Ho, Carly Monardo, Carly Weir, carlysher, Carol Sevin, Carolina Aguila, Caroline Gelber, Caroline H. Phillips, Caroline Orlin, Caroline R. Heinbuch, Caroline Thompson, CarolineCharlie, Carrie Ann Wartmann, Carrie Haase, Carson Hawks, Case Dykstra, Casey Pitts and Amit Sabnis, Cassandra Okerhjelm, Cassi Henning, Cassidy Sillars, Cat Hester, Catherine, Catherine Findorak, Catherine Neal, Catherine Nygren, Catherine Payzant, Catie Mac, cats, Cecilia Provvedini, Cesium, Chanel Choi, Charles Howard Williamson, Charlie Tidwell, Charlotte Grace, Charlotte Gund, Charlotte Lowey, Chelsea Dauser, Chelsea Leigh Brown, Chelsea Stearns, Cheryl DF09, Chesca Uy, Chilly Winters, Chloe Bragg, Chloe Kiddon, Chloe Prosser, Chloe Reepe-Kaiser, Chris "Christophales" Herring, Chris & Katherine, Chris Bowen, Chris Burnette, Chris Carrico, Chris Chase, Chris Curry, Chris Davis, Chris Hathway, Chris Hinton, Chris Hopkins, Chris Jensen, Chris Kurszewski, Chris McLaren, Chris Pai, Chris Raghoobar, Chris Roberts, Chris Sarnowski, Chris Schulz, Chris Webster, Christian Cerilles, Christian Ort, Christie Lynn Paquay, Christina Cavaleri, Christina Laverentz, Christina Michela, Christina Miller, Christine Bernat, Christine R. Becker, Christine Ventura, Christophe Pettus, Christopher "Cookie" Koncilja, Christopher "King Banana Slug" Simons, Christopher Arnold, Christopher Damico, Christopher J Weber, Chrys Anastasi, Chynna Cordevilla, Cian Booth, Claire Kelly, Claire Stevenson, Clara Lauterwasser, Clare Murray, Claudine LeBosquain, Cody Ferguson, Cody J. Peterson, Cody Y., Cole, Colin, colin & mle, Colin Smith, Colin Young, Colleen & Ken, Collette Lee, Connor J P, Corey A. Cook, Corey Grajkowski, Corey Rogers, Corky LaVallee, Cormick Dineen, Cory Bevilacqua, Cory Copeland, Courtney McDermott, Courtney McGrath, Courtney Summers, Craven P, Crissy Calhoun, Cristina Merrit, Andrew Prange and Dan Prange, Crystal Titus, Damien, Dan Blackman, Dan Clark, Dan Frank, Dan Olson, Dan Reed, Dan Shimkus, Dan Smart, DAN!, Dana Bubulj, Dana M., Danfuzz Bornstein, Dani Cash, Dani Jones, Dani Legault, Dani Sanchez, Danie Roux, Daniel Garcia, Daniel Hsu, Daniel Osborne, Daniel Perelman, Daniel Rathbun, Daniel Schoenbach, Daniel Weiskopf, Daniel Weissbarth, Danielle Cabrera, Danielle Callie Fox, Danielle Fortin, Danielle Hughson, Danielle Janmaat, Danielle M. Cregan, danielle reiss, Danielle Rhoades, Danielle Rogers, Dann Malihom, Danny Cannan, Danny Dravland, Danny Mears, Dante Shepherd, Darren Hinger, Darzie Ryba, Dave, Dave Harmon, Dave Stebbins, David, David, David, David

Scott Rubel, Scottie Macleod, Sean, Sean Bouchard, Sean Byram, Sean Caulfield, Sean Clay, Sean Hexed, Sean Maciel, Seán Peter Smythe, Sean Swanky Doodle Gilligan, Sean T Gill, Sean Wentzel, Seoirse Rue Gleeson Melis, SERGIO SANCHEZ, Seth Benjamin, Seth Carbon, Seth Tubman-Watkins, sevenhelz, the malfunctioning robot, SGardner+JFerguson, Shane Steinert, Shannon Lea Hartzler, Shannon Turner, Shari Hill Sweet, Sharyn & Michael Brady, shawn, Shawn, Shawn Brenneman, Shawna C. Romero, Sheilagh-Marie Stacey, Shirine Sajjadi, Shivaun M. Robinson, Sian, Michael, Heidegger and Mocha Dart, Sidney Dritz, Simon Pook, Simon Walling, SK Gaski, Skye Forster, Sloan Duncan, SMCS, Smelliot Lee, Sol H. Jacobsen, Sol Roter, Sophie Mackey, Sparrow, Spike Jensen, Spinelli, Stacey, Stacey Butler, Stacey S. Haysler, Stef, Stef Stein, Stefan Voinea, Stefanie Garber, Steph Lim, Stephanie, Stephanie Ang, Stephanie Goddard, Stephanie Highfield, Stephanie Smith Rust, Stephanie Trimboli, Stephen "Sven" Kay, Steve Collins, Steven Bentley, Steven Lauterwasser, Stevena Labadie, Stevie Rae, Stone Chin, stormagnet, Sunshine, Suru Riikka, Susan Adsett, Susan and Bryant, Susan L. Sandenaw, Susan Marie Groppi, Susannah Macrae, Susanne Salehi, Suz, Svend Andersen, Sydne McCluskey, Sydney Yang, t s, jr, Taen (Suzon) Hardy, Tamara A, Tamás Prileszky, Tanya K. Osborne, Taryn Germaine Orlemann, Tasha Donnelly, Taylor, Taylor and Jessica Davis, Taylor Johns, Tea Kew, Teague Peace, TEAMKILLTOM, Tegan Hendrickson, Tennille Oppen, Terence, Clare & Aeryn Chua, Teresa Flour Lamb, Terry Callan, Terry Robinson, Tes Sensibaugh, Tessa Alexanian, the chimerical collective, The Gibbs Family, The Konstas Kids, The Mighty Alex Gotay, the Miratrices, Thea Moura, Thilina, Thomas Eckenfels, Thomas Werner, Thorne & Erin Lawler, TiFaRi, Tiffany Huang, Tiffany Myers, Tiffany Teen, Tim, Tim Arsenault, Tim G. Patterson, Timothy Geier, Timothy Winn, TJ Dickson, Tobias Powell, Tobias V. Langhoff, Todd Palmer, Tom Beverly, tom dissonance, Tom Harris, Tom Hickerson, tom joyce, Tomoko Iwata, Toni Siimes, Tony Heugh, Tony Iamunno, Toyfulskerl, Tracey Gaughran, Traci Beatovic, Tracie Henderson, Travis M Hicks, Trevor Baxter, Trevor Mischief Hook, Trevor Sthen, Trine Rasmussen, Tristan Ham, Tushar Nene, Ty Hudecki, Ty Schwartz, Tyler Campbell, Tyler Giffin, Tyler Kelley, Tyler Mortenson, typodactyl, Ulreh Vogt, Uncle Benny, Urška Bajec & Aljaž Košmerlj, Usman Choudry, Valerie Carisma, Vallerie Rose Perrault, Vance Lockton, Vanessa Lynch, Varsenik Wilson, Vegard Stenhjem Hagen, Vernon Putman, Veronica Superfly Jones, Vi Truong, Victoria Ellis, Victoria M. Schneider, Victoria Pyle, Violet Farraday, Virginia Garbero, Vitorio Miliano, vudvris., W. H. Barkley, Waider, Wardell Tindaan, Webster, Wes Price, Wheat Wheatington, Whiskeypants, Wil Hart, Wiley Davis, Will Kaufman, Will Lesieutre, Will McVicker, Will Walawender, William Heathcote, William Kyle Smith, William Mawdsley, William Pietri, William T. Grindle, Xavier RS, Xian O'Brien, Xiao Fan, Zach, Zachary Knudsen, Zachary Rose, Zack Guzman, Zack Johnson, Zak Kaveney, Zander Horn, Zeke Wickstein, Zenia McAllister, Zenith, Zoe Adele, Zoë Aizenman, Zoe Aleshire, ZuckerNelson Adventure, _Mark_, .nos., Pammenter, (none, thank you), (The) Foubert Family, ~trent rehberger, @petulapetula

GLOSSARY

Sometimes my reflection needs a stern talking-to. Hello, it's a brand new day. Today you can start right over. Forget old obligations, you can throw away all your old hopes, too. Why are you still wishing on that same old star? That was somebody else's star. You're brand new today! Dream a new dream, dipshit!

Broken Heart: A misnomer, like calling an empty box of cereal 'broken' after you've enjoyed every bowl.

Dead Parents: Usually in the second half of your book, but a few copies have this sprinkled in the early chapters. We're so sorry.

Struggle: Just because you have only seen the inside of your own house doesn't mean everyone else is living in a cardboard set.

Perfect: Anything you think of briefly enough can be perfect.

Lesbians: They can remember your face if you mistreat them. They watch you from power lines. You will never be safe again.

Sadness: An ever-replenished resource.

Secrets: Something to keep hidden in your mouth.

Mouth: Warm and safe. A place for secrets to grow.

Lips: The little lock on your secret diary.

Tongue: The key.

Heretics: Tired of putting money in the collection plate.

Postage: Please pass this note to Derek for me. Here's fifty cents for your trouble.

Halloween: The one true High Holy Day.

Cat: As fluffy as the Second Coming.

Baby Doom: We don't know. If you're smart, you won't know either.

Love: See pages 12b, 14b, 16b, 17, 18b, 21b, 22, 29a, 29b, 30a, 30b, 35b, 38b, 39, and on and on until you give up. Please don't give up.

Freedom: This is your destiny.

Wings: The tools of destiny.

Magic: It's a magical world!

Magic: It's a sufficiently technologically advanced world!

Soul: Turn to pages 14a, 41b, for a once-in-a-lifetime business offer!

Redemption: While supplies last.

Inevitable Ruin: Certainly not evitable.

Family: All happy families are alike? Whoever wrote that never saw *The Texas Chainsaw Massacre*.

Sweet Pranks: Have some good natured fun at the expense of the people you love, today! You'll get a good story out of it, and good stories are the buttresses of relationships.
Punk Rock: Put a pin in your love. Sew a patch on your love! When your love is new, put it on and roll around in the dirt til it looks right! Love, love, love!

Retail: 16a, 34b,, 45b, on and on and on, like love's evil twin.

Revolution: See retail for the origins of this.

Adventure: Take a look in the mirror!

Laughter: Medicine. Addictive. Worth ruining your life over.

Emily Horne: Takes the photographs. Will one day save us all.

Joey Comeau: A horrible warning. Or a good example? I can't tell.

Ryan North: A wonderful friend. Speaks almost entirely in Dad Jokes.

Mike Lecky: Keeps telling the same "Pumpkin Spice Latte is back?" joke but we like him anyway.

Maggie Dort: The invisible beating heart of A Softer World? Is it…is it under the floorboards?

Pumpkin Spice Latte: is back!?! I warned that motherfucker.

Lust: Every-goddamn-where you look, sometimes. Sometimes nowhere.

Gender: I'll have a smoothie, please.

Obsession: We started writing down what pages had 'obsession' comics, but I lost interest.

Superpower: My superpower is writing indices that do not do what indices are supposed to do.

Christmas: Wake up early day, a habit from when you were so small.

Beauty: In somebody's eyes, probably. I wonder where they got to?

Queer: Mister, we ARE the weirdos.

Zombie: Slow, fast, I'm the guy with the gun.

Doctor: Play to win.

Lonely: Only these.

Hope: Worse than death.

Death: Worse than hope.

Suicide: A permanent solution to an infinite series of ever-worsening temporary problems.

Dirty Pictures: You can be young forever.

Regrets: NONE

Awkward Love: All elbows and knees of the heart. Kisses with the mouths too open. Blushing yourself to sleep with a big smile.

Emily Horne saw a gator in the wild for the first time this spring, and it was totally worth it! With her friend Tim Maly, she wrote a book about surveillance called *The Inspection House*. Now that *A Softer World* is over, she's going to concentrate on her five interests: brewing fine beers, petting fluffy cats, thinking about headless Jeremy Benthams, looking at photos of astronauts, and grilling delicious pineapples.

Joey is a firm believer in the idea that if you can't be a good example, you have an obligation to be a horrible warning. He has a degree in linguistics which really only comes in handy when smart-asses try to correct his grammar at parties. He's the author of various novels and books, including *Lockpick Pornography*, *Overqualified*, *One Bloody Thing After Another*, and others! He likes candy. Sour candies mostly. Fuzzy peaches. Sour grapes. But man, yeah. Candy.